SNOW

Lisbeth Mark and Babs Lefrak

A Lefrak Press Book
Perigee Books

A Perigee Book
Published by The Berkley Publishing Group
200 Madison Avenue
New York, NY 10016

Copyright © 1995 by The Lefrak Press, Ltd.
Text copyright © 1995 by Lisbeth Mark and Babs Lefrak
Book design and illustrations by Nancy Novick
Cover photo © 1993 by Willard Clay/FPG International
Cover design by James R. Harris

First edition: December 1995
Published simultaneously in Canada

Library of Congress Cataloging-in-Publication Data
    Mark, Lisbeth.
        Snow: Lisbeth Mark and Babs Lefrak.—1st ed.
            p. cm.
        "A Perigee book",
        ISBN 0-399-52166-6 (pbk. : alk. paper)
        1. Snow. I. Lefrak, Babs. II. Title.
    GB2603.7.M37 1995
    551.57 ′ 84—dc20   95-14811

Printed in the United States of America
10 9 8 7 6 5 4 3 2 1

Contents

INTRODUCTION

Snow is good. It feeds reservoirs in the winter for use during dry summer months. It insulates delicate roots against bitterly cold winter temperatures so that flowers and vegetables can sprout in the spring. Snow is bad. It's responsible for countless fender-benders, broken ankles and sore muscles from skids, slips and shovelling mishaps. Most people tend to have one view or the other.

Snow lovers are those ruddy-cheeked outdoor fiends who start waxing their skis in September and tune up their four-wheel drives in anticipation of early winter. They look forward to the first descent of the white stuff from the heavens. Those others who are, shall we say, less enthusiastic about icy temperatures and frozen precipitation, lay in supplies of rock salt and tune up the snow blower in preparation for the siege that is snowfall.

This book will help you, depending on how you look at it, get to know your friend a bit better, or gird you against your enemy.

CHAPTER 1

SNOW TECH

Snow is not just frozen rain. After all, weather people forecast freezing rain and that's not snow. A snowflake is born when one or more ice crystals develop from atmospheric moisture in below-freezing air.

The Birth and Journey of Snowflakes

At the heart of each ice crystal is a tiny particle (called a nucleus) upon which moisture can collect and solidify. Usually a speck of dust is enough to get things started. The crystals grow in size and number, and when they start sticking to one another, snowflakes are born.

It all starts in the clouds, although sometimes, if the air is supercooled enough, ice crystals can grow in clear air, from the water vapor floating around. But in most cases, it takes clouds like nimbostratus (layered, water-droplet clouds that hover in a gray layer close to the ground); cumulus congestus (dome-shaped clouds with definite shapes that contain water droplets) or cumulonimbus (the grandaddies of all storm clouds—big, black and full of water). They provide enough water for snow to form.

The amount of moisture in the atmosphere and the temperature at which they are formed determines the shape and complexity of the snow crystals. The colder the air, the less moisture it can sustain, so the warmer the air, the larger the crystals can grow. Snow that develops at extremely low temperatures (around -20°F or lower), where the moisture supply is also very low, usually forms long pencil-shaped crystals. At temperatures just below 0°F, most snow crystals form flat, six-sided plates. The six-sided quality is a reflection of the atomic structure of the molecules that make up water (oxygen and hydrogen) when it's frozen.

The most beautiful snowflakes fall when temperatures are

between 0° and 20°F and the ground temperature is around 15° to 20°F. These large, complex flakes are the kind you really want to catch on your parka sleeve to examine. When the temperature gets much warmer than this, the weight of the crystals causes them to splinter apart into "needles."

Even under the best temperature conditions, snowflakes get knocked around a lot during their fall to the ground by the wind, air currents and collisions with other flakes. So they're pretty irregular-looking by the time they reach the ground. When enough snowflakes get together and become heavy enough to start falling from the clouds, you've got a snowstorm.

When the ground temperature is below about 15°F, the snow is that light fluffy stuff that's really good for nothing. Trying to shovel it is futile, since it just blows all over. You can't get it to stick together for a decent snowball. Above 15°F, things start to cook. Since the dendrite (from the Greek work for "branched" or "treelike") flakes stick to themselves and then to anything vaguely horizontal, the winter wonderland effect starts to kick in. The closer to freezing (32°F) it gets, the more the flakes start to melt and stick to anything, including lampposts, the dog or your nose.

Are No Two Snowflakes Alike?

It's hard to say if any two snowflakes are exactly alike because there are so many variables involved. For two snowflakes to be exact twins, they would have had to form under precisely the same conditions and fall to earth in precisely the same way.

Wilson Bentley decided to find out, in the 1880s, if he could find two twin snowflakes. On his farm in Jericho, Vermont, using amateur photographic skills, he began collecting snowflakes on film. Bentley painstakingly photographed over five thousand snowflakes (using a box camera, black-and-white film and a microscope he'd received for his fifteenth birthday), over the course of forty-six winters. Several thousand of his photographs were published in 1931, in a book titled *Snow Crystals*. While the book was used to identify and classify snowflake types, Bentley sometimes edited his photographs for artistic purposes, sadly limiting the book's scientific value, and he never did find two exactly alike.

The fact that virtually all snowflakes are six-sided was recorded in 1611 by German mathematician Johannes Kepler (though scholars from China before Kepler wrote of snow having properties associated with the number six). In 1665, Robert Hooke, an Englishman, may have been the first to study snow through a microscope. In the eighteenth and nineteenth centuries, whaling captains and literate explorers wrote about snow crystals, and Japanese royalty drew and wrote about snow "blossoms."

A Russian meteorologist, Shuchukevich, identified 246 different snow crystals one winter, and in the 1930s a Japanese meteorologist named Ukishiro Nakaya categorized seventy-nine types of snow crystals along with weird ones he called mavericks.

The International Commission on Snow and Ice developed a snowflake classification system in 1951. Along with crystals, ice pellets, hail and graupel, the commission acknowledged seven basic forms:

Stellar crystals form in clouds of about 24° to 14° F. and, without a wind to knock off their delicate points, fall to earth as six-pointed stars.

Hexagonal plates are six-sided and form at 32° to 9°F. They develop in very still air and sometimes link up with stellar crystals to form larger, intricate flakes.

Spatial dendrites are like stellar crystals except their shape is less regular. They form in massive, moist clouds and, if magnified, look like flowers.

Irregular crystals are an amalgam of crystals that have descended during blustery weather.

Needles are like tiny icicles, roughly the size of grains of rice. The needles are hexagonal spears and form in moderately cold climates.

Columns, like needles, are hexagonal shafts that resemble quartz crystals. They occur in temperatures of less than 12°F. in high, thinner clouds. Columns can act as prisms, creating halo effects in the sky.

Capped columns are larger columns that have collided with hexagonal plates. The plates form little caps on the ends of the columns.

By the way, when ski resorts tell you that they're "making snow," they're not entirely correct. Their snow-blowing guns are really spewing tons of ice pellets that resemble snow when they're piled up on the ground. That's why "granular" conditions are so prevalent during a slow snow season.

Snow Warnings

Snowstorms come in all different shapes and sizes. From the smallest non-sticking flurry to the blizzard of '88-sized inundation, weather forecasters never seem to get it right. In fact, meteorologists are now much better than they used to be when it comes to predicting the amount of snow that will fall on a given area. Sophisticated radar, satellites and computer projections enable them to zero in on the path and intensity of a storm. Snow-watches and warnings prepare us for the amount of white stuff that is likely to hit the ground and stay there. Forecasters generally use the same terminology to describe the type of snowfall that will occur. By knowing these terms, you can keep one step ahead of the elements.

Snow *flurries* are very light, intermittent snow showers—kind of like drizzle if it were raining instead of snowing. There's usually very little, if any, accumulation associated with flurries (sometimes called a *dusting* if the snow does stick), although flurries can reduce visibility to less than one-eighth of a mile on roads and highways.

Just plain *snow,* without a qualifier like intermittent or occasional, usually means that the snowfall will be pretty steady and will last a few hours. It doesn't necessarily mean that it will be very heavy, just continual. Accumulations from this kind of snowfall are usually less than four inches.

When the forecast calls for *heavy snow,* your smiling weatherperson is telling you that at least four inches will fall in a twelve-hour period, or six inches within a twenty-four-hour time frame. Of course, if you live in a very snowy area of the country, expect at least six inches as the cutoff for heavy snow. Similarly, if you live in the Sunbelt, an inch or two can be considered a crippling blizzard.

A *snow squall* is a short, intense snowfall with gusty winds. It's a lot like a passing summer thundershower—in and out quickly but with a lot of precipitation. These brief storms are most common in the mountains and in the lee of the Great Lakes, where the atmosphere picks up warm moist air from the lakes and then dumps massive quantities of snow on Buffalo, Cleveland and surrounding areas.

When the weatherperson predicts a *blizzard* coming, take heed. These babies are dangerous. A blizzard means that you can expect not only copious amounts of snow (usually the fine, powdery stuff), but also strong winds and low temperatures. The winds whip around the snow, making visibility minimal, and often the snow accumulates so fast that the plows can't keep up with it. The wind and snow disorient people foolish enough to walk out into the stuff. Folks have been lost walking to the corner for milk or negotiating the ten yards to the garage. Drifts are caused by the wind blowing both falling and fallen snow into big, sloping piles. The wind can even sculpt snow bridges over streams. Yes, it's picturesque—*after* the blizzard is over. While it's at full bore, stay inside!

Avalanches

A heavy snowstorm can cause one of the most dreaded results of weather: an avalanche. Avalanches are most common when new snow settles on the crust of old snowfalls, most often on steep mountain slopes. The new snow slips off the old and gains tremendous speed during its descent down the mountain. It is so powerful that it creates an "avalanche wind" in front of it that can uproot trees and demolish buildings even before the actual snow from the crushing wave hits.

If the old snow has a crust hardened by sunlight or frozen rain, all it takes is about twelve inches of new snow to create an avalanche, especially on slopes of twenty-five degrees or more. Blizzards that begin when the snow is dry but end with wetter snow are also likely to set the stage for an avalanche.

There are two basic kinds of avalanche: *loose-snow* (which starts from one point and widens as it descends) and *slab* (a massive chunk of snow that breaks off and thunders down the mountain, leaving behind what is known as a *crown wall*). Even tiny avalanches can indicate danger to come.

Avalanches cause so much destruction that snow hydrologists (scientists who study the effects of snow) are constantly monitoring snow when the conditions are ripe and issuing warnings to protect people in avalanche-prone areas. Ski areas employ experienced mountaineers and skiers to test the snow several times a day. Aside from taking into account snowfall, layering, wind and temperature, they conduct field tests. For example, in the Rutschblock test, pressure is applied (sometimes by the edge of a ski) to a column of snow to test its stability. Ski resorts occasionally elect to set off explosive charges to trigger controlled avalanches to protect against unexpected ones.

See Chapter 7 for more on avalanches and avalanche safety.

Glaciers

Glaciers are formed by the repeated melting and freezing of millions of dainty snowflakes, which turns them into massive ice forms. Many glaciers develop in the shape of mountains, and their own weight forces them to spread out, usually in a downhill manner. Anything in the glacier's path is pushed aside or run over by the enormous power and weight of the ice. Fortunately, glaciers move very slowly—often mere inches in a year.

Glacial movement sculpted the earth as we know it. As glaciers moved through the ages (most notably through ice ages), they scraped away at topsoil and soft rock and left bare bedrock behind. Actually, glaciers don't really move across the ground, but rather they expand as the weight of new snow and ice flattens out the ice below—sort of like what happens when you press down on a burger while it's grilling. Valleys and lakes are formed by gashes the ice creates in softer rock, while the piles of displaced rock and soil create hills. The advances and retreats of glaciers are responsible for much of the earth's topography. An out-of-place hill? A gigantic boulder in the middle of nowhere? The culprit was probably a glacier.

During an ice age more than ten thousand years ago, the great plains of North America were formed by the sheer accumulated weight of the ice sheets that accompanied the glaciers. One of the best examples of the work glaciers can do is the Great Lakes. Pre-Ice Age, there were no major inland bodies of water in North America. Post-Ice Age, Lake Superior became the world's largest freshwater lake.

10 percent of the Earth is covered by glaciers, mostly at the poles. The largest and oldest glaciers are in the Antarctic and are more than three miles thick. These monsters have been growing for more than 15 million years! Under the dense snowpack of Antarctica, there are entire mountain ranges that haven't seen the light of day in aeons.

Glaciers aren't just in the Arctic and Antarctic. One of the two peaks of Mount Kilimanjaro in Africa is topped with a glacier. And the Alps in Europe are full of small glaciers that have survived since the Ice Ages thousands of years ago.

Icebergs

Eventually, part of the creeping glacier hits a coastline, breaks off and falls into the water. *Voilà*—an iceberg is born. Ten to fifteen thousand icebergs drop off Greenland and Canada and hit the waters of the Arctic Ocean each year. They take about two years to melt away, but only about four hundred per year actually survive the journey into the Atlantic. (Although rare, an occasional rogue iceberg has been known to make it as far south as Bermuda.) Odds of a serious iceberg making its way down into the shipping lanes of the Atlantic Ocean are very slim, which is one of the reasons why the demise of the *Titanic* was such a surprise.

There's a lot more activity in the Antarctic. Over a trillion tons of ice is dumped into the sea each year, and these babies are huge—up to five miles long and fifteen stories tall! When they drop into the ocean, you can expect them to survive ten years before they melt away. *Growlers* are sedan-sized, while *bergy bits* can be as big as a barn.

Icebergs can be white, green, or blue to the eye, and some have measured more than two hundred miles at their widest points. Others have an altitude of three hundred feet. They float because the air trapped inside makes them buoyant. That's just the tip of the iceberg, so to speak. The greatest mass is submerged, just like an ice cube in a glass of water.

Icebergs are now a business. Chunks are harvested, covered in giant plastic wrap and dragged to places like the Middle East, to supply fresh water, if they don't melt along the way.

Snowed Under

* The largest snowflakes on record might have occurred during a snowfall on January 28, 1887 near Fort Keogh, Montana. A report in an issue of Monthly Weather Review claimed that the snowflakes were "larger than milk pans" and measured some fifteen inches in diameter and some eight inches thick. The mega-flakes fell over several square miles. The largest snowflake officially recorded measured four inches in diameter. Most snow crystals are about one-eighth inch in diameter.

* Vincent Joseph Schaefer produced artificial snow from a real cloud on November 13, 1946. Soaring over Mount Greylock, in Massachusetts, he tossed pellets of dry ice from his plane from an altitude of fourteen thousand feet. While the snow evaporated before it actually hit the ground, he is credited as being the first snowfaker.

* Gray icy patches, resembling snow, have been photographed on Mars, where temperatures can dip to -310°F.

- While the sky and sunlight can tint snow to the eye, red or pink snow is created by microscopic algae that grows in clumps in the snow. Other forms of algae have been credited with creating yellow, green and blue snow.

- Explorers in Antarctica discovered that extreme dips in temperature (below -50°F.) made skiing impossible. At that temperature, ice crystals come down more like sandpaper than a skiable surface. Skis and sled runners stick on the unmeltable crystals rather than slightly melting them and gliding over the surface. Crunch!

- When measuring snowfall, thirty inches of dry snow or six inches of wet snow is about the same as one inch of rain.

- During any ordinary winter in places like New England, North Dakota, Finland, Siberia or British Columbia, some million crystals of snow fall and cover each two-foot-square area with ten inches of snow.

- About 48 million square miles of the Earth are covered year-round with snow or ice.

CHAPTER 2

THE SNOWS OF TIME

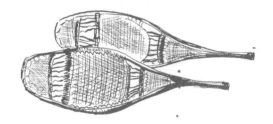

Snow has figured into some famous historical events as both a hero and a villain. And history has changed the way we perceive snow and those who have battled it.

Ancient Snow

During his neverending quest to expand his empire, Alexander the Great set his sights on India in 330 B.C. However, the snowy peaks of the various mountain ranges that protect the northern and eastern borders of that country proved too much of a frustration.

At the start of the Second Punic War, Hannibal invaded Italy from Spain to expand the Holy Roman Empire, crossing the snowy Alps with elephants—his preferred mode of transport. Hannibal and his ill-suited pachyderms suffered terribly when trying to cross the Alps. He called snow the "white enemy." After all, ski lifts hadn't been installed yet in 216 B.C.

Colonial Snow

Who would have thought that the Pilgrims, aside from taking credit for being the "first" on several scores, were also among the first Europeans to taste American snow? When the Mayflower landed at Plymouth Rock in 1620, the Pilgrims had to row their boats ashore through a snowstorm.

Another highlight from American snow history is Valley Forge, a spot on the Schuylkill River just outside of Philadelphia. Close your eyes and you can see the image of our brave (though untrained) minutemen hunkering down in the woods of Pennsylvania, suffering through snow, hunger, nasty windchill and George Washington's moody visage. The winter of 1777-78 was a key period for the American Revolution. Philadelphia had been captured by the British, and the

patriots stationed outside the city at Valley Forge suffered miserably from hunger and the cold; the quar-
termasters had miscalculated the need for
food and blankets. When they did real-
ize what they needed, Congress
refused to grant Washington's pleas for
supplies. The silver lining is that
Generals Steuben and Lafayette drilled the
men through the winter so that, by June
1778, they were a disciplined military force to
be reckoned with. Good news also came from Saratoga—General
Horatio Gates defeated the redcoats and turned the tide of the war.

At least Washington and his army could take comfort in the
fact that the winter would eventually come to an end. But almost three
decades later, that didn't happen.

Mount Tambora, a volcano in Indonesia, erupted in 1815,
sending a cloud of dust, ash and cinders into the upper atmosphere. The
volcanic dust reflected the heat from the sun back into space and the
weird result was a year without a summer.

Snow fell on the northeastern United States and parts of

Europe throughout the summer of 1816, killing newly planted crops and dooming the region to a winter of hunger and a spring of desperation. May had been cold, but a warm spell in early June encouraged farmers to plant. Then a bitter wind arose on June 6 and 7, and snow fell, drifting to twenty inches in Danville, Vermont. Four weeks of good weather encouraged replanting, but by July 4, another cold wave had wiped out corn, beans and squash. Farmers burned their hay to try to save their corn. Again warmth returned, and again farmers replanted. On August 21 snow fell and lasted all winter. Over the next year, farming families left their land in record numbers to move south or to work in factories and on the Erie Canal.

Westward Snowbound

Snow frequently got in the way of westward expansion across the continent and literally froze industry in its tracks. The laying of the Central Pacific Railroad through the Sierra Nevadas in the 1860s progressed until the Golden Spike was driven into the dirt in 1869. The architects of the cross-country line didn't take into account the problem of serious snow on the tracks. Cars and plows were derailed. Avalanches closed down parts of the route. Travelers often had to get out and walk around snowdrifts and the stuff strewn about by avalanches. Trains were often days late, blocked by falling snow and rocks.

The Klondike Gold Rush of 1897-98 called out for men and women to risk everything for a chance at instant wealth. Most ventured through the Alaska panhandle to the headwaters of the Yukon River. Many lost their supplies and some their lives as they were caught by fierce snowfall on their way to the gold fields. The Royal Canadian Mounted Police were kept busy tracking lost would-be miners and entrepreneurs. The Mounties, no fools, demanded that each person who crossed the border into British Columbia had to have a year's supply of food and provisions—and they were there to collect duty on everything. But those who tried to avoid paying duty by crossing the frontier regretted it. Whole teams of men, animals and sleds disappeared into crevasses or under avalanches.

Conquering Snow

The early decades of the twentieth century were the golden age of polar exploration. American Robert Peary and his assistant Matthew Henson, along with a team of fifty Eskimos, traveled by dogsled to the North Pole in 1909 and provided an increased impetus for teams from Britain, Germany, Norway, Japan and Australia to compete to reach the South Pole first.

Norwegian explorer Roald Amundsen, who had already successfully been the first to navigate the Northwest Passage in 1906, assembled a team of four crew members for his assault on the South Pole. Over the desolate terrain of Antarctica, they launched their expedition on October 20, 1911 with fifty-two dogs, four sleds and a four-month supply of food. Twelve days later, on November 1, British explorer Robert F. Scott left McMurdo Sound on the coast of Antarctica with a five-man team, motorized sleds and ponies to haul their supplies. He believed that his party would more than make up the time lost to Amundsen's primitive dogsleds.

Despite the Antarctic summer, the weather was particularly bad. Scott's team had to abandon the motorized sleds when low temperatures caused gas and oil to thicken and seize up the engines. The ponies were not physically suited to the Antarctic conditions and died from exposure and exhaustion long before the team was even close to its destination. Their dogs died soon after. The five men ultimately had to haul their supplies themselves as they traversed the terrain on skis and snowshoes.

Scott finally did reach the Pole on January 18, 1912. When he arrived, he found the Norwegian flag implanted at the site where Amundsen had made his camp—thirty-five days earlier. On the return trip, Scott's provisions were exhausted. Three months after reaching the Pole, Scott and his companions died during a blizzard. When their remains were found the following November, a year after they originally set out, they were only eleven miles from the supply depot.

Snow has also served as an effective weapon in combat. When the Austrian and Italian armies faced each other in the Austrian Alps during World War I, more deaths were caused by man-made avalanches that were part of the battle strategy than by shells and bullets. More than sixteen thousand casualties were reported in one four-day period.

SNOWED UNDER

* It's believed that the first snow shovel was unearthed from a bog in Russia. Some six thousand years old, the shovel's blade was made from a carved section of an elk's antler. Archaeologists believe the antler piece was tied to a handle made of wood or bone.

* Good King Wenceslaus who looked out "when the snow lay round about, deep and crisp and even," was a Bohemian king martyred in the fourteenth century.

* Gustavus Adolphus, King of Sweden from 1611 to 1632, was nicknamed the Snow King when he visited Vienna. The joke was he could keep himself together in snowy climes but melted and disappeared when he approached warmer soil.

The Humble Snowshoe

The snowshoe was the first device to serve as a foot extender to make travel over snow or ice easier. It originated in Central Asia around 4000 B.C. and is one of man's oldest inventions.

Snowshoes helped aboriginal people migrate all over the northern hemisphere (across what is now the Bering Strait). The eastward-bound peoples favored and retained the use of showshoes. The westward-bound peoples (those who ended up in Europe, especially Scandinavia) developed them into skis. That's the reason why until the twentieth century, skiing was more popular as a means of getting around in Europe than in North America (where people were still using snowshoes).

Indians (not Eskimos) perfected the snowshoe design. The Athapascans of the American and Canadian west coast and the Algonquins of the Ottawa and St. Lawrence River valley took the basic bearpaw design and added hundreds of patterns to suit all possible conditions. When the French started to colonize the St. Lawrence River valley in the 1600s, they adopted snowshoes from the Indians. The French used them to their advantage in the French and Indian Wars against the British, and during westward expansion of the United States, snowshoes were standard issue to soldiers and militiamen.

Snowstorms and Blizzards

Blizzards are basically snowstorms that have gone berserk. They generally combine the worst winter conditions—low temperatures, raging winds and high levels of precipitation—into a sudden thrashing of the countryside. They often come on suddenly and with great intensity. Famous blizzards include the following:

April 1846. A group of ninety settlers known as the Donner Party were trapped in record-deep snow at Truckee Pass, California en route to Sacramento. Forty-two died; others turned to cannibalism to survive before they were rescued.

Mid-March 1888. The Mother of All Blizzards set off cyclones as far south as Georgia because of a low-pressure system up north. One cyclone spun out over the Atlantic and then set its sights on New York City. The cyclone was met by an icy blast from Canada and the worst blizzard folks could remember was born. For the next two days, area residents were held in the grip of snowdrifts and violent winds. New York City and New England were buried under drifts fifteen feet high. One hundred ninety-eight ships were sunk or damaged. Telegraph service was cut off between New York, Philadelphia, Boston and Washington. Thirty-foot snowdrifts blocked trains for days, and the

East River was choked with ice floes and proved impassable. In total, eight hundred people died in the Northeast, two hundred of them in New York City alone. Thirty years later, The Society of Blizzard Men was formed by survivors of the blizzard of '88 and continued to meet regularly to trade stories of the great one.

November 1913. Two hundred thirty people died as storms dumped thirty-five inches over the Great Lakes; eight ships were wrecked on Lake Huron alone.

February 1956. Storms and bitter cold swept the globe from New England to Siberia; around the world, nine hundred seven died. Continuous snow for ninety-two hours caused millions of dollars of damage in Texas and New Mexico.

January 1977. A blizzard descended upon southern Ontario and western New York State. Thousands of people in Buffalo were trapped in offices, schools, shops and such for up to three days.

1986. One of the heaviest snowfall years on record in Europe. During March, most of the continent was paralyzed by heavy snows and bitter cold, and a severe blizzard, with winds reaching 210 miles per hour, hit Great Britain.

Extreme Snow

* The snowiest spot on record in North America is Ranier Paradise Ranger Station in Washington, where, in the winter of 1971-72, a total of 1,122 inches of snow fell. Their average snowfall is 575 inches per year.

* A most remarkable snowstorm occurred in Mount Shasta Ski Bowl in California from February 13 through 19, 1959 when 189 inches of the stuff fell. This is a United States record for the greatest single snowfall.

* The deepest snow measured in the United States was 451 inches at Tamarack, California, on March 11, 1911.

* Before motorized snowplows, cities used heavy rollers pulled by teams of oxen to flatten the snow on major roads and paths. It was actually easier to travel on sleighs over snow in the winter than on rutted, rocky, sometimes muddy roads during other times of the year. Towns and cities really didn't need to plow their streets until streetcars were developed and the tracks needed to be cleared for the trollies to run.

CHAPTER 3

SNOW GLOBE

People from different cultures around the world have developed singular ways of acknowledging snow. They've invented legends to explain it, created festivals to celebrate it and even worked out ways to consume it.

Proverbially Snow

Proverbs from different spots on the globe reflect how snow is perceived. Some treat snow kindly, as a harbinger of good things to come in the spring. A French proverb, for instance, declares, "A year of

29

snow, a year of plenty" or "A snowy year, a fruitful year." Others are less optimistic. The Norwegians are prone to declare, "Snow is the peasant's wealth."

"Corn hides itself in snow as old men in furs." This English proverb suggests the folly of dwelling on one's glory days.

The Scots have a different take. Like those folks who watch birds, groundhogs and woolly worms for clues, they believe "Many haws [hedge berries], many snows."

The Turks, ever optimistic, remind us, "However much snow falls, still it does not endure the summer."

In the you-can't-get-something-from-nothing category, Italians aver, "From snow, whether cooked or pounded, you will get nothing but water."

Several proverbians warn that snow is ephemeral and does melt. So bury the evidence under a rock slide.

"Dirt under snow sun discovers" is from the English.

"What lay hidden under snow comes to light in the end" is a Dutch proverb.

This Chinese proverb seems to warn that it's best to mind one's own business and to shovel one's own driveway: "Let each sweep the snow from before his own door; let him not be concerned about the frost on his neighbor's tiles."

Leave it to the oft-snowbound Swedes to be pragmatic: "No one thinks of the snow that fell last year."

By the way, a quintessentially American viewpoint is that it snowed more when we were kids. Wrong. We were shorter then. It just seemed like more snow.

Mythically Snow

Where snow plays an important role, it enters the realm of legends. A Japanese folktale, for example, tells of Yukionne (Snow Woman or Snow Maiden), a spirit of death. Depicted as pale and serene, she would lead those lost in snowstorms to sleep and eventually to die. After calming them with a kind of soothing lullaby, she'd blow her fatal icy breath on them.

According to Native American Chinook lore, Wah-Kah-Nee was the "drifting maiden." The Chinook story is told of an endless winter in the Pacific Northwest. Afraid that spring would never come again, the tribe council met to determine who could have brought upon them this horrible fate. An elder told that an endless winter could be the result of someone having murdered birds needlessly. A small girl was discovered crying, and confessed that she had, in fact, thrown a stone which had mistakenly hit a bird and killed it. She was left on a block of ice as a sacrifice to the winter spirits. Instantly, spring returned. When winter came again the next year, a block of ice was spotted floating by. Inside was the body of the girl. Rescued and revived, she was able to walk through blizzards barefoot and communicate with the spirits of winter ever after.

In Nordic mythology, snow is an ancient man known as King Snaer. His daughters are Snowstorm, Thick Snow and Thin Snow. Ullr is a winter god, a skilled warrior, who loved Skadi (for whom Scandinavia is named), a goddess who skied and snowshoed through her mountain kingdom. After her unsuccessful first marriage to Njord, a sea god, she and Ullr found each other and frolicked in the snow side by side for all eternity.

German, Austrian and Swiss folktales share a character named Frau Holle (or, sometimes, Holda). An old wife, Frau Holle, was said to circle the world in her wagon between December 25 and January 6 and to make it snow by shaking out her feather bed. For these twelve days, superstitious folk didn't use wheels—rotary motion was forbidden. Sleighs were used instead.

Snow-covered mountain areas are the homes of some legendary figures. The Tibetan White Goddess of Heaven, gNam-Iha dkar-mo, is said to live on Mount Everest. Pana is a sky woman who cares for the souls of the dead according to Inuit lore. Her home is the sky, which is full of holes that form stars. Through the holes she shakes rain, hail and snow. "The Man from Snowy River", an Australian classic, is the story of an inspired horseman from the Snowy Mountains of New South Wales.

Yeti is the Sherpa (Himalayan guide) name of the "Abominable Snowman" whose tracks in the snow were first publicized in 1951 by a British expedition scaling Mount Everest. The footprints were eighteen inches by fifteen inches. Bigfoot, or Sasquatch—the Indian name— is believed to lurk in the North American woods, and his tracks were first spotted in 1811.

Mount Snow

What would mountains be without snow? More aptly, where would snow be without mountains? Some snowcapped highlights include the following:

Tanzania's Mount Kilimanjaro, immortalized by Ernest

Hemingway, is Africa's tallest mountain and is also an extinct volcano. Its two peaks are Kibo (19,340 feet high) and Mawenzi (17,564 feet high). Kilimanjaro is the world's tallest mountain that is not part of a mountain range.

Mount Fuji is also a volcanic peak and rises 12,389 feet above Honshu, Japan. Surrounded by the Fuji-Hakone-Izu National Park, Mount Fuji (also known as Fujiyama or Fuji-san) is considered sacred in the Shinto religion and is a destination for religious pilgrimages. The legendary Fuji has been the subject of writers, poets and artists for centuries.

Chomo-Lungma (the "Mother Goddess of the Land") is the highest mountain in the world at 29,028 feet. It sits on the border of Nepal and Tibet in the central Himalayan mountain range. While its English name, Mount Everest, honors a British explorer and surveyor who never made it to the top, it was Tenzing Norkay and Sir Edmund Hillary who are credited with being the first to reach the summit in 1953.

The highest point in North America is Mount McKinley (20,320 feet high)—also known as Denali—in the Alaskan Range. More than half of the mountain is permanently covered by snowfields.

Hudson Stuck is thought to have been the first to scale its forbidding heights, in 1913.

The Alps are probably the most romanticized range of mountains in the world. Their highest summit is Mount Blanc, which lies on the borders of France, Switzerland and Italy and is some 15,770 feet tall. Other notables in the range are the Matterhorn and the Eiger.

Snow Bowl

In the kitchen, snow can be an ingredient or the desired effect. Snow cones are made from shaved ice and flavored syrup. They are best eaten in a paper cone at the circus, on the boardwalk or strolling down the carnival midway (*after* your ride on the tilt-a-whirl). They're also a welcomed relief to inner city summer heat.

Snow eggs *(oeufs a la neige)* are a dessert made from meringue. Whipped egg whites are shaped with the back of a spoon to look like peaks of snow. Poached in sweetened milk, they are served with a custard sauce.

Snow is a name often applied to a light and fluffy dessert, usually served cold. Unlike a soufflé, it's not that hard to make.

SUSAN'S LEMON SNOW

3/4 cup sugar
1 1/2 tablespoons butter
2 teaspoons grated lemon rind
3 eggs (separated)
3 tablespoons all-purpose flour
1/4 cup lemon juice
1 cup milk

Cream together the sugar, butter and lemon rind. Add the egg yolks and beat thoroughly. Gradually add the flour and juice and milk to the mixture. In a separate bowl, beat the egg whites until stiff. Fold them into the mixture.

Place the finished batter in a seven-inch-diameter baking dish or soufflé dish that has been set in a pan filled with about one inch of hot water. Bake in the water bath for approximately one hour or until set. Cool in refrigerator for several hours or overnight before serving. Serves 4 - 6 people. Oranges can be substituted for the lemons.

Maple syrup snow, a snow snow cone, can be made by heating maple syrup on the stove to 232°F (use a candy thermometer), then pouring it over a bowl of clean snow. Scoop up the taffy-like concoction into a cup or, better yet, an ice cream cone. This is what is meant by "sugaring off" in maple syrup country.

"Sugar snow," incidentally, is not a sweet treat. It is a term coined by farmers in New England to describe a late spring snow which would slow the flow of sap, thus allowing them more time to collect maple sugar for syrup.

Snow Fests

The Sapporo Snow Festival, the most spectacular of all snow extravaganzas, has been held annually since 1950 on the island of Hokkaido, Japan's northernmost main island. Each mid-February, along the Odori-Koen Promenade, the festival features elaborate statues and fantastic ice palaces carved from ice and packed snow that is trucked in from the surrounding mountains. More than two million visitors are drawn to the event, and snow carvers from around the world come to exhibit their skills.

Winter festivals around the United States feature torchlit ski runs; contests on skis, sleds, toboggans, dogsleds, snowmobiles, ice skates; parades and fireworks; beauty pageants and talent shows; food and drink; dances and balls; ice and snow sculpture contests. With names like Frostbite Follies and Winter Carnival, they serve to amuse and divert during the monotony of northern winters. Some American celebrations include the following:

Ullr Fest. The third week in January in Breckenridge, Colorado.

Winterskol. The third weekend of January in Snowmass Village, Colorado.

The White River Winter Rendezvous. The last weekend of January through the first week of February in Meeker, Colorado.

The Saint Paul Winter Carnival. The last weekend in January through the first weekend in February in St. Paul, Minnesota.

The McCall Winter Carnival. The last weekend in January through the first weekend in February in McCall, Idaho.

The Grangeville Winter Festival. The third weekend in January in Grangeville, Idaho.

Snow Flora

Stunted by blizzards and a very short growing season, willow trees in the northern tundra areas of the globe only grow to about six inches in height.

Snowballs are not just something kids throw. They are a kind of shrub which blooms in the spring. The flower is a puffball with small white blossoms. Another shrub, called a snowberry, and an annual called snow-on-the-mountain (also known, less attractively, as ghost-weed) derive their names from the whiteness of the real stuff. Other snow flora include an herb called a snowdrop and a Mediterranean plant called a snowflake. The bell-shaped blossoms of these are delicate and, not surprisingly, white.

SNOWED UNDER

* A halo around a winter moon may be a sign that the white stuff is on its way. The effect is really caused by ice crystals in the air that bend the reflected light of the moon.

* It can get so cold in places like Siberia that boiling water poured from a kettle will turn into ice before it hits the ground.

* The interior of Antarctica gets very little snow. There, even though it's the coldest place on Earth, there is so little moisture in the atmosphere that snow falls in the form of ice crystals—with an annual precipitation equal to less than two inches of water (about what the Sahara gets).

* Snow control in the United States uses one-sixth of the world's total supply of salt.

* Snowy is the name of Tintin's faithful dog in the English editions of the eponymous French comic books. (In the original French, he's Milou.)

* *Nanook* is the Inuit word for polar bear.

CHAPTER 4

SNOW PACK

While people deal with it, animals around the world have ingeniously learned to adapt to snow and occasionally thrive in it. Snow is indeed an excellent blanket. It keeps the cold and wind out.

Snow Motion

Some animals hibernate, while others, who stay awake on a somewhat normal schedule, work hard all winter just getting by.

Toads can submerge themselves in mud and, closing their eyes, nose and mouth, take in minute amounts of air through their skin.

They can stay that way for hours and be unaffected by the cold. Snakes, raccoons, skunks, groundhogs and bats also hibernate. Voles, field mice, muskrats and beavers are wide awake and work on survival all winter long. Some small critters, like mice and voles, dig caves and tunnels in the snow for shelter and to avoid becoming prey. There are three classifications for north country animals: *chionophobes* (unable to adapt to snow); *chionophores* (able to survive snow); *chionophiles* (dependent upon snow to survive). *Chion* is from the Greek word for snow.

Snowshoe hares (or rabbits) turn from reddish brown to white in the winter, and their wide bunny feet help them negotiate the snow. They inhabit the northern United States and Canada.

Caribou and reindeer migrate to where the snow doesn't completely cover the ground. Deer like to winter in a dense grove of evergreens. They look for tall conifers with thick tops to protect them from the wind and snowfall. Lushly needled branches keep the snow from reaching the ground. Called deeryards, these areas allow the deer to move around, find food and be protected from snowstorms. Deer can also dig in the snow with their fur-covered muzzles, sniffing out plants. They also pack down trails in the snow.

Snow's the Name

Snow fleas, found atop snow in parts of Canada and the United States in late winter, are capable of jumping sixty times their own minuscule height. Snow worms are also alive and wriggling in some snowbanks, so look before you snack on surface snow. Some insects survive the snow by manufacturing glycerol, a type of alcohol that works like antifreeze.

The snow goose is a North American gray goose that does its breeding in the Arctic.

The snow leopard lives around the treeline in the mountains of central Asia. The large cat sports a whitish, long-haired coat and a very long tail. Its markings are a remarkable pattern of yellow, brown and black.

The snow monkey, also known as a macaque, is from Japan. Unlike its cousins, this primate doesn't mind straying from the equator. The snow monkey's long fur keeps it comfortable at high altitudes, although these animals are known to warm themselves in hot springs they find in the mountains.

The snowy owl is one of the heaviest of the owls, weighing in at upwards of 4.5 pounds. These birds have a wingspan of approximately five feet and create their nests on the ground with feathers. Native to the northern states and all of Canada, they dine on lemmings, Arctic hares and ptarmigan, ground-dwelling Arctic birds. The snowy owl rarely hoots, except occasionally during mating season. Aside from being excellent camouflage against the snow, its white hair cells help maintain body heat.

The snow crab is one of two crabs found in the northern Pacific Ocean. This crustacean is especially edible and is harvested in Alaska for distribution throughout the lower forty-eight states.

Snowbirds

While some birds fly south for the winter, others simply change their eating habits. The spruce grouse, for example, flies up into the tree-tops and eats berries and buds. When too tired to hold on any longer, this bird plops down and rests in a nest of snow it makes for itself. Ruffed grouse dive headlong into snowbanks to root around for plants to eat.

Whooper swans catch air under their feathers to trap body heat. Then they hunker down and wait for the snows to pass.

The ptarmigan is a gifted camouflage artist whose feathers are white in the winter and russet in the summer. Its feet grow wider and longer in the fall. The middle talon elongates and feathers grow all around the bird's foot, adapting it into a kind of snowshoe. The pressure of the ptarmigan's footstep on the snow is thus reduced by 60 percent.

The snowbird is a gray-colored junco, a finchlike bird native to the eastern United States. It appears with the first snow. "Snowbird" is also the nickname given by native Floridians to a Northerner who flies south for the winter.

The only thing snowy about the snowy egret, a large, white bird found in America, is its white feathers. It has a black bill, black legs and yellow feet.

Penguins—Dressed for Snow

Those nattily clad penguins can stand on ice floes because they have papillae (little pads) on their feet. Papillae keep their toes from freezing. If the temperature takes a serious nosedive, penguins can rock back onto their tails to keep their tootsies toasty.

Emperors, the largest type of penguin, are the ultimate in

selfless parents. Once the female has laid her large egg, she heads off to hunt fish in the open water to regain her strength. But first, her mate takes custody of the egg. He rolls it gently onto his feet and folds it under a flap of skin just beneath his tummy. To conserve strength, warmth and energy, the male penguins gather together, their backs to the icy wind and their eggs on their feet. Sixty-three days (give or take twenty-four hours) later, the females return just in time for hatching. Each takes her hatchling on her feet, under her belly flap. She'll share the fish she's been noshing with her chick.

Now it's Dad's turn. He stumbles out to sea, half-starved. Sometimes he's so weak he slides along on his belly in the snow. For three weeks he'll bulk up, then he returns to his chick and once again takes over, sharing his food with his offspring. The parents continue this tag-team feeding for several weeks until the chick has its gray down and no longer requires Mom and Dad's body heat to survive the cold. Come summer, after a few weeks in the colony's nursery, the chicks acquire their waterproof feathers and head north to eat, grow and bulk up for next winter with all the other penguins.

Penguins are expert sledders, using their bodies to glide over packed snow. They do it recreationally.

And why are penguins always formally attired? Protection, of course. When they're looking for food in the water, predators on the surface can't see them well because their black backs blend in with the inky depths. Predators below see only the white of their bellies, which blends in with the light coming through the water. It's great camouflage!

In the Snow

How do some species manage in the Arctic freeze? Polar bears are made for it. They are strong swimmers, and because of their dense, oily outer fur, bubble-trapping underfur and thick layer of fat, they stay afloat and their skin remains dry. And under that heavy white coat, their skin is black, to conduct the warmth of the sun. Like snow-shoe hares, polar bears get good traction on snow and ice because of the hair on the underside of their paws.

When not digging around for plants or bird eggs, they are wily hunters, waiting for hours beside a seal's breathing hole. To stalk a seal on the ice, the bear will flatten itself against the ice and edge forward using its massive hind paws. Cubs are trained to sit motionless some distance from a blowhole while their mama hunts. Polar bears can smell prey across miles or under densely packed snow.

In winter, sables grow extra underfur, while a marten's underfur grows longer, trapping warm air.

The Antarctic fulmar, a large seabird, avoids becoming prey by letting snow drift around it and sitting motionless in a warm bed of the white stuff.

Mountain goats make their way through the snow in very woolly coats that grow longer during winter months.

The ermine, a short-tailed weasel that's brown in summer, all but disappears in the winter, when its fur becomes white (save for a blacked-tipped tail). The dark-tipped tail is part of the ermine's survival strategy. Larger predators notice and attack the black end rather than the white body.

The lemming is the only rodent that has fur that changes color (from brown to white) in the winter.

Sleep Snowly

Some animals just choose to sleep away the winter. By lowering their metabolism rates, they are unaffected by the cold, and spend the winter in a state of rest.

Male and female brown bears hibernate separately. They

don't need a cave; more often they curl up in a den made under the roots of a fallen tree, or in a hollow spot in the ground. Some make nests from sticks and leaves, while others dig out beds in the sides of hills. Some bears have been known to curl up under the porch of a vacation home. Their thick coat and a layer of fat keep them from freezing.

Mama bears give birth during the hibernation period but don't sleep through it. On the contrary, they are up often tending to the tiny cubs.

Usually resigned to deal with the elements, polar bears don't den—unless pregnant. In October a mother-to-be digs a cave in a snowbank and uses her body to warm and smooth the entrance and walls. Or she may simply lie down and let the snow cover her. Her cubs are protected from Arctic blasts for several months nursing and nestled beside their mother.

Gray squirrels like to spend their winters in a cavity inside a big, old tree. Several males will share a den together, as will younger females. Older females prefer to hole up alone. Red squirrels, who tend to den alone, get cozy in snow tunnels or under a tangle of roots.

Snow Dogs

Proving just how good a friend they are, dogs have hauled their fair share of people and supplies through the snow. Samoyeds (often known for having one blue and one brown eye) and Siberian huskies are renowned for their performance in the snow.

Originally most Native Americans used snowshoes and pulled small sleds to transport firewood, food and animal pelts them-

selves. But the Inuit peoples of the far North developed dogsleds to carry their loads. With the smooth runners of the sleds propelled by swift-footed dogs, the Inuit were able to cover far more ground than they could by foot. The dogs also helped as trackers and retreivers during hunting expeditions. The only downside was that they needed to be fed, which meant extra food weight on the sleds.

On a dogsled team, the lead dog is harnassed alone. This dog is the heart and soul of the team, actually guiding, encouraging and directing the other dogs along the trail. The lead dog is trained to reserve its energy so that at the end of the run, when the dogs are tired, the lead dog inspires them with its stamina. To demonstrate their status, lead dogs are given special privileges, such as being unharnassed and fed first.

The Iditarod Dog Sled Race, established in 1973, covers the gruelling route from Anchorage to Nome (1,163 miles) and is run each March. It commemorates the 1925 mission that delivered lifesaving vaccine to the citizens of Nome during a particularly virulent diphtheria epidemic.

Balto was the Siberian husky who led a dogsled team through Arctic terrain and a raging blizzard for the final leg of the original trip to Nome. The driver of the team told reporters, "I couldn't see the trail. Many times I couldn't even see my dogs, so blinding was the gale. I gave Balto, my lead dog, his head and trusted to him. He never once faltered. It was Balto who led the way. The credit is his."

Balto died as a result of the expedition, but his heroic

exploits are commemorated by a statue in New York's Central Park, the only statue of a dog in New York City.

Saint Bernards have a highly developed sense of smell and can find people trapped in or under snow. Their massive paws dig people out and the dogs are trained to lie beside victims to keep them warm until a search party arrives.

The breed is named for the Saint Bernard hospice of Saint Gotthard Pass in the Alps. There, Saint Augustine monks kept the dogs for companionship, for their ability to plow through the snow and for defense against bandits. And the dog's nose made it valuable when the monks went in search of lost travelers or to rescue those felled by avalanches. Although commonly depicted with kegs of brandy around their necks, Saint Bernards have never been dispatched by rescue teams into a snowstorm for cocktail hour.

Chinook are a breed of sled dog founded by Arthur Walden in the late 1910s. Developed for New England winters, they almost vanished as a breed in the sixties but are making a slow comeback. Tawny-colored, with the look of a mastiff and German shepherd mix, Chinook made a name for themselves in Arctic expeditions and by beating out an established Canadian team in the first Eastern International Sled Dog Derby in 1922.

The white, woolly Great Pyrenees was also bred for snowy mountains as guard dogs for sheep. They have double dew claws (claws near their ankles) for grabbing which makes them extra sure-footed in the snow.

Bernese mountain dogs were originally used to haul carts full of craftsmen's wares around the town of Berne, Switzerland. Known as eager workers who required little supervision, they soon flourished throughout the Alps. As carts were replaced by motorized transportation, their popularity dwindled, but they are still kept as loyal companions in cold climes.

Newfoundlands have often been the lifesaving companions of fishermen during the cold North Atlantic winters. Massively strong and equipped with a heavy coat, they have frequently rescued their masters from the icy waters. They have also been used to drag sledges across the snow in the depths of winter and are entrusted with protecting home and hearth during the fishermen's long absences.

Like Siberian huskies and Samoyeds, the Alaskan malamute was originally bred as a harness dog in the Arctic. It evolved through selective breeding by the Eskimos—that is, the only bloodlines that were sustained were those of dogs that could endure the rigors of the gruelling work and the biting cold of the Arctic. Stronger than its smaller cousin the husky, the malamute can pull heavy sleds long distances without complaint.

CHAPTER 5
SNOW SPORTS

As long as there has been snow, there have been people trying to have fun in it—often competitively. Perhaps inspired by belly-surfing penguins or drift-diving grouse, someone, somewhere, strapped on a pair of planks and screeched the ancient equivalent of *"cowabunga"* while speeding down the snow-covered slopes.

Scandinavians have transported themselves on ski-like con-traptions for centuries, from about 3000 B.C. Being able to move around quickly on snow was a necessity for hunters, soldiers and anyone who didn't want to spend most of the year trapped indoors. To get around, folks skied on elongated "snowshoes" carved from wood.

Time to Hit the Slopes

Alpine (or downhill) skiing, named for, lo, the Alps, is a relatively new form of gliding atop snow, which became popular in the nineteenth century. Alpine inspired the hybrids such as downhill racing, slalom, *randonnée* (a French term for mountain ski touring on downhill skis), mogul and bump skiing and snowboarding.

Nordic (or cross-country or free-heel) skiing is an ancient mode of transportation developed in Norway and Sweden. Classical (long, diagonal strides) and freestyle (a variety of skatinglike motions) are the two techniques most commonly used. *Telemark* combines a little downhill with cross-country, and the skis for this discipline normally have metal edges. Nordic skiing also inspired ski jumping and backcountry wilderness skiing or ski touring.

What are the differences in the equipment? The basic nordic ski is slimmer and lighter; the boot is flexible, and the skier's heel is not fixed to the ski. The alpine variety is more stable and the ski boot is stiffer; the ski boot is locked down onto the ski with a mechanical binding, and the heel doesn't lift.

The oldest ski is thought to be the Hoting ski, found in a bog near the Swedish village of Hoting. The wooden ski measures 3.5 feet in length and is thought to be more than four thousand years old. Cave pictures in Sweden and Norway depict hunters and warriors on skis, some with ski poles.

Skiing for sport evolved in the United States some 150 years ago. Twelve-foot-long hickory planks brought over by Scandinavian immigrants were called snowshoes. They were used by miners working the mountains around California and in the Rockies. Informal competition, ski clubs and racing teams soon evolved, in the 1850s, as recreational activities.

In 1868, Swede Sondre Norheim beat out all the contenders at a ski competition in what is now Oslo. While everyone slid, slipped and floundered on ten-foot-long skis attached with leather toe loops, Norheim developed shorter skis and came up with heel anchors. His revolutionary turn, still used by some skiers, is a maneuver in which both the knees bend and one ski is thrust forward. Called the Telemark (like the method mentioned above) turn in honor of Norheim's hometown, it's a very stable way of changing direction. Norheim is considered the granddaddy of modern downhill skiing, having made so many marked improvements in what he considered less a method of transportation and more a fun sport.

After hearing about Arctic explorations on skis, an Austrian named Matthias Zdarsky was motivated to try it. He is credited with developing a different turn from the Telemark. Using a staff and applying weight to the downhill ski, which he stemmed to the side and pointed in the general direction he was aiming for, Zdarsky invented the "stem christiana" or "stem christie" turn (now known as a parallel or stem turn). He wrote what is thought to be the first book on alpine skiing technique in 1896.

John "Snowshoe" Thompson, who came to California from Norway in 1851 to seek his fortune in the gold fields, is credited with bringing skis out west for the first time. His wooden, homemade twenty-five-pound skis enabled him to carry the mail (sometimes as much as one hundred pounds worth) over the snow-covered Sierra Nevadas in midwinter. Before Thompson, all communication between California and points east had to wait until spring. Old Snowshoe carried the mail from 1856 through 1872, when the recently completed railroad replaced him. He retired claiming he was owed some five thousand dollars by the government for his postal work. Though he never collected, his skis and snowshoes helped popularize winter sports in the mining camps and throughout the snowbound West. Too bad the Donner party of 1846-47 didn't know about them.

Skiing became immensely popular with tourists to the Alps in the 1920s. An enthusiast named Sir Arnold Lonn organized friendly downhill competitions using flag poles. Competitors, in the game he called slalom, had to zigzag through a field of flags. The International Ski Federation added downhill racing and slalom to the ski running and jumping contests in 1930. Six years later they were included for the first time in the Olympic Games.

Another boon was Marius Eriksen's improvements to the ski. He used laminated wood with steel edges for better flexibility and control. Marius's son, Stein, proved to be an international champion and stylist. Howard Head, an aircraft engineer from Baltimore, introduced skis of layered aluminum around a plywood core. They were light, durable and much more steerable than wood. However, metal skis were not allowed in competition until the 1960 Olympics in Squaw Valley. Modern skis are a high-tech mix of everything from carbon fibers to ceramic. Compared to the bulkiness of those early wooden planks, today's skis literally turn on a snowflake.

Surfing on Snow

Snowboarding is the fastest growing sport in America, now making up over 10 percent of all downhill skiing. Less technical than downhill skiing and requiring less equipment, it's a combination of surfing, skateboarding and skiing with a definite emphasis on personal style. Competition is held in both slalom and freestyle events. Slalom races run against the clock through an intricate series of gates not unlike slalom ski courses. Freestylers compete in events including the pipeline or tube, which requires competitors to perform maneuvers while dropping down almost straight walls of snow. The U.S. Open snowboarding competition is held annually in Breckenridge, Colorado, and attracts the world's premiere boarders.

The Winter Olympics

The first Winter Olympics actually sponsored by the International Olympic Committee were held in Chamonix, France, in 1924. They included ski jumping, cross-country races, bobsledding and skating events. Two Winter Olympics have suffered from uncooperative weather. In Lake Placid in 1932, snow had to be trucked in from Canada. During the 1988 Calgary Olympics, warm Chinook winds kept melting what little natural snow there was. Artificial snow (really tiny ice pellets) filled in the bare spots.

Sport by Sport

The *biathlon,* a combination sport of rifle shooting and cross-country skiing, was inspired by military drills organized by the Norwegian army. Competitors race on their skis with a .22-caliber small-bore rifle slung across their backs. Small targets are placed at distances of fifty meters, and competitors shoot from either a standing or prone position.

Having skied against the clock, competitors must be able to reduce their pulse rates instantly (to about 140 beats per minute) in order to be able to aim with steady hands. After firing a specified number of times, they then speed off to the next target. Missed targets mean a time penalty or racing an extra loop.

Men race 10 or 20 kilometers or as a four-man relay team, each member skiing 7.5 kilometers. Women participate in a 7.5- or 15-kilometer race as individuals or in a three-woman relay team with each member skiing 7.5 kilometers.

One of the fastest ways down a mountain is in a *bobsled*. Bobsleds are the sports cars of the Olympics (they were one of the original Winter Olympic sports) because of their speed and the expense of their design. National teams spend millions of dollars on getting just the right combination of aerodynamics, steering sensitivity and lightweight materials to propel their sleds down refrigerated courses at speeds over seventy miles per hour. The runners of the sleds are so precious that during international competitions drivers have been known to sleep with them! Competition is in two-man or four-man sleds, with the driver controlling the course down the run using two ropes that steer the front runners. The brakeman only applies the brake at the end of the run, and he helps the team get the best possible running start at the top of the course. Standings are awarded according to combined times of four runs. Bobsledding is one of the few Olympic sports for which there is no women's competition.

While bobsleds at least have some protection for their riders, *luge* riders fly down a course just a bit shorter than a bobsled run feet-first, atop what looks like a child's sled. Steering is a matter of subtly transferring weight from side to side, and speed is controlled by sliding front or back on the sled. A wipeout is spectacular and dangerous—definitely the agony of defeat. For world and Olympic competition, runners cannot be farther than eighteen inches apart and may not be heated before a race. (Warmed runners slide more easily through the ice.) Riders (known as sliders to the cognoscenti) hurl themselves down the course in singles and doubles competition.

Alpine events include Downhill, Slalom, Giant Slalom, Super Giant Slalom (the Super G) and Alpine Combined for both men and women.

The *Downhill,* arguably the most dramatic of the Alpine events, is won or lost on a single run. Speed is everything, and competitors zoom along in excess of 80 miles per hour as they hurtle down the fall line of the mountain.

The other Alpine events depend on turning technique instead of raw guts. *Slalom* requires more control as competitors thread their way in and out of gates (two poles) that have been set in intricate turns down the mountain. If a gate is missed, the skier is disqualified. The competition is decided upon the total score of two runs on two different courses. The *Giant Slalom* is simply a longer course with wider turns. The *Super G* combines the daredevil mentality of downhill speed with the technique necessary to make the gates. Finally, the *Alpine Combined* is a two-day event incorporating a downhill run and two slaloms.

Freestyle Skiing became a medal event in Albertville in 1992. Aerials (acrobatic jumps and somersaults) and Moguls (bump skiing) are Olympic events while Ballet, considered a freestyle event at other competitions, is not yet on the Olympic menu. In *Aerials,* skiers are awarded points for air (height and distance), form (execution) and landing. In *Moguls,* the skier must maintain control and a clean line while completing two aerial moves (judged on height, distance, landing, execution and degree of difficulty) while racing against time. The aerial maneuvers have entertaining names such as the daffy, the zadnik and the back scratcher.

Nordic Skiing events include Cross-country, Ski Jumping and Nordic Combined. *Cross-country* races embrace two styles of skiing: classical (requiring a diagonal stride) and freestyle (no restrictions and incorporating the speedy "skating" style). Because these events are strongly influenced by weather and the quality of the snow, equipment changes as frequently as the conditions. Wax (which enables the skis to glide over the snow more smoothly) and other accessories may be handed off to a racer on the course, but must be applied by the racer to his skis without aid. A skier must allow the right of way if about to be passed, and if the passer has shouted out, "Track!"

There are ten-and thirty-kilometer classicals, a fifty-kilometer freestyle, a four-man relay in which each man races ten kilometers (two using the classical technique and two freestyle), and a combined pursuit (ten-kilometer classical one day and fifteen-kilometer freestyle the next).

Ski Jumps, scored on distance and style, take place on what are differentiated as a normal hill (sixty meters) and a large hill (ninety meters). Medals are awarded in both events, and finish is determined by the combined total of four jumps. Individuals usually compete on both hills, and teams compete on the large hill. Women do not compete in the Ski Jump.

In the *Nordic Combined* events, competitors ski jump on a normal hill one day and cross-country race fifteen kilometers (ten if on a three-man team) the next.

Women's Nordic Skiing includes five- and fifteen-kilometer classicals, thirty kilometers freestyle, a combined pursuit (five kilometers classicals and ten freestyle) and a four-woman relay where each member races five kilometers.

Snowed Under

* The official record for the fastest skier is held by frenchman Philippe Goitschel who was timed going 145.161 miles per hour on April 21, 1993.

* Tony Sailer of Austria (in 1956) and Jean-Claude Killy of France (in 1968) are the only two Olympic alpine skiers to win three gold medals (in the downhill, the slalom and giant slalom) in one Olympic Games.

* In 1991, the Snow Bowl in Camden, Maine, proclaimed itself New England's longest (and perhaps scariest) toboggan run. It's got a 440-foot-long ice-coated chute where tobogganers have been clocked at 80 mph.

* The first rope tow to transport skiers to the top of a ski run was erected in Shawbridge, Quebec—powered by a four-cylinder car engine. The first American rope tow, powered by a Ford, was at Gilbert's Hill in Woodstock, Vermont. It was built in 1934 by David Dodd and Frank Stillwell. A normal trip took two minutes to get from bottom to top. The operator, however, delighted in running the rope at twenty-five miles per hour and thereby tossing skiers into the air at the summit.

* Averell Harriman opened the Sun Valley ski resort in Idaho in 1936, along with the world's first chair lift. Hollywood stars made the sport glamorous and the chair lifts made the mountains accessible. The lifts were even outfitted with lap blankets to keep the celebrities toasty on their way up to the top of the mountain.

CHAPTER 6

Snow Culture

Writers, poets, directors, artists and composers quite regularly call upon the image of snow to instantly transmit a mood to their readers and viewers. It's been used for centuries to set the scene, convey emotions (from desolation to childish fun) and add a tinge of excitement or quiet reflection to movies, stories and paintings.

Snow Lit

The Call of the Wild by Jack London. The story of the dog Buck, who is stolen from his comfortable home and pressed into service as a sled dog. He finally breaks away and becomes the leader of a pack of dogs in the snowy wilds of Alaska.

69

The Snows of Kilimanjaro by Ernest Hemingway. A hard-drinking writer heads to Africa and reflects on his life before he dies. In a dream, he sees a giant, mythic frozen leopard on the summit of the mountain.

War and Peace by Leo Tolstoy. More than five hundred characters, dozens of battle scenes, Napoleon's invasion of Russia and all that snow as a backdrop!

"The Dead" by James Joyce. The final of the Dubliners collection of stories. After attending his elderly aunts' Christmas dance, the main character, Gabriel Conway, looks out at the snowy night and reflects on death.

Silas Marner by George Eliot. On her way to meet her secret husband, Molly Ferren dies in a snowstorm. Her children, including little daughter Eppie, wander into the cottage of a lonely weaver (Marner). He raises the girl as his own, and sixteen years later, when she has the opportunity to live with her rich father, Eppie chooses to stay with Marner.

Ethan Frome by Edith Wharton. It seems like the whole book takes place in a snowstorm, but the major event is a sledding accident for Ethan and his mistress, Mattie. He ends up with a wicked limp and takes care of his crippled girlfriend—while both continue to live with his wife, who looks like a saint next to the nagging Mattie.

Women in Love by D. H. Lawrence. At the end of their vacation, after Gerald's relationship with Gudrun ends and he rejects the friendship of Rupert, Gerald commits suicide by walking up into the snowbound Tyrolian mountains.

Snow-Bound, A Winter Idyll by John Greenleaf Whittier. This long prose poem harkens back to Whittier's snowbound boyhood on his father's farm in New England and winter times with his family.

The Waste Land by T. S. Eliot. Certainly one of the most famous (and controversial) poems of the twentieth century, this long work frequently evokes images of snow to illustrate the struggles of the human soul seeking redemption.

Notable Snow Quotes

"I don't know when the snow began to set in; but I know that we were changing horses somewhere when I heard the guard remark that 'The old lady up in the sky was picking her geese pretty hard to-day,' then, indeed, I found the white down falling fast and thick."

—Charles Dickens, "The Holly-Tree"

"As thick as the snowflakes on a winter's day, when all-wise Jove has begun to snow, showing his power to mortals. Stilling the winds, he pours snow down upon the ground, so that the tops of the lofty mountains, the sharp peaks, the lotus-plains, and man's productive labors, are buried deep. It is scattered over the hoary sea, lakes, and shores; but the wave, it approaches, controls it; everything else is wrapped up beneath, when the storm of Jove rages with fury."

—Homer, *The Illiad*

"I love snow, and all the forms
Of the radiant frost."

—Percy Bysshe Shelley, "Song"

But pleasures are like poppies spread—
You seize the flow'r, its bloom is shed;
Or like the snow falls in the river—
A moment white—then melts forever.

—Robert Burns, "Tam o' Shanter"

"This is the Hour of Lead—
Remembered, if outlived,
As Freezing persons, recollect the Snow—
First—Chill—then Stupor—then the letting go."

—Emily Dickinson, "After Great Pain, a Formal Feeling Comes"

In the bleak mid-winter
  Frosty wind made moan,
Earth stood hard as iron,
  Water like a stone;
Snow had fallen, snow on snow
  Snow on snow,
In the bleak mid-winter,
  Long ago.

—Christine Rossetti, "A Christmas Carol"

Full knee-deep lies the winter snow,
And the winter winds are wearily sighing;
Toll ye the church-bell sad and slow,
And tread softly and speak low, For the old year lays a-dying.
—Alfred, Lord Tennyson, "The Death of the Old Year"

"Be thou as chaste as ice, as pure as snow, thou shall not
escape calumny."

—Shakespeare, *Hamlet*

"Come night! come, Romeo! come, thou day in night!
For thou wilt lie upon the wings of night,
Whiter than new snow on a raven's back."

—Shakespeare, *Romeo and Juliet*

"The frost performs its secret ministry,
unhelped by any wind."

—Samuel Taylor Coleridge, "Frost at Midnight"

"Nature is full of genius, full of the divinity; so that not a
snowflake escapes its fashioning hand."

—Henry David Thoreau, *Journal*

"The same law that shapes the earth-star shapes the snow-star.
As surely as the petals of a flower are fixed, each of these
countless snow-stars comes whirling to earth."

—Henry David Thoreau, *Journal*

The north wind doth blow,
And we shall have snow,
And what will the robin do then,
Poor thing?
He'll sit in a barn,
And keep wimself warm,
And hide his head under his wing,
Poor thing!

   —Anonymous Nursery Rhyme, "The North Wind Doth Blow"

"To mimic in slow structures, stone by stone,
Built in an age, the mad wind's nightwork,
The frolic architecture of the snow."

—Ralph Waldo Emerson, "The Snow-Storm"

"No snowflake in an avalanche ever feels responsible."

—Stanislaw Jerzy Lec, *More Unkempt Thoughts*

Mary had a little lamb,
Its fleece was white as snow,
And everywhere that Mary went,
The lamb was sure to go.
—Sarah Josepha Hale, "Mary's Lamb"

"Mais ou sont les neiges d'antan?" [But where are the snows of yesteryear?]
—Francois Villon, *Le Grand Testament*

"When a cloud freezes, there is snow."
—Aristotle

In the Bible, snow is credited for its whiteness and beauty. There is mention of morsels of ice, frost, hailstones and hoarfrost, as well as a snowcap on Mount Hermon. Job speculated that snow came from storehouses in the sky, and that water hardened like cast metal under a cold wind—the breath of God.

Snow Cliché Users Anonymous

It's impossible not to, you'll excuse the expression, fall into snowy metaphor. Earle Stanley Gardner may win the award for the most eager snow-clichéer. The urge just piles up, and writers find themselves shoveling out from under the turns of phrase. Before we lose our drift, herewith are some examples:

"Clean as snow, white as snow." (Ray Bradbury)
"He was light as snow." "She was cold as snow." (Ross Macdonald)
"Their relations were as pure as driven snow." (John Dos Passos)
"We haven't got the chance of a snowball in hell." (James Joyce)
"I used to be Snow White, but I drifted." (Mae West)

Snow Art

Although many artists from many cultures have explored the image of falling and settled snow (the sacred snow-capped Mount Fuji is a recurring subject in Japanese works), it was the Impressionists who most examined snow in new and different ways. They took their canvases out into the snow (earlier schools made sketches of landscapes outdoors but painted in their studios). They were also keen on playing with the effect of light, shadow and texture on snow, which enabled them to reveal all the qualities of white, snowy vistas. Three artists in particular, Claude Monet, Camille Pissarro and Alfred Sisley, produced some of the most beautiful snow paintings, including Monet's *Boulevard Capucines,* Sisley's *Snow at Louveciennes* and Pissarro's *The Outer Bridge, Snow Effect.*

Late nineteenth-century American artists like Grandma Moses and the members of the so-called "Ashcan" school (including John Sloan, Maurice Prendergast, William Glackens and Ernest Lawson) used snow scenes as subjects for their realistic paintings.

Arguably no artists did more to glorify and romanticize snow than the American lithographers Nathaniel Currier and James Merritt Ives. Their nineteenth-century landscapes captured the quintessential peaceful New England winter countryside, complete with horse-drawn sleighs and playing children.

Snow Dance

Probably the most famous reference to snow in dance and classical music is the "Dance of the Snowflakes" in Tchaikovsky's *The Nutcracker.* Usually performed by ballerinas in diaphonous, snowflake-like tutus, to music scored for strings, the dance truly captures the flight of snowflakes as they whirl through the air to the ground.

Snow Movies

Filmmakers have successfully manipulated snow both as a backdrop and as a protagonist. They have used snow to set the scene, establish a mood, propel the action, enhance the drama and move their audiences. A surefire way to add some atmosphere to a film is to set at least part of it in snow country. For example, think of Audrey Hepburn's first meeting with Cary Grant in *Charade,* or the moment when William Hurt releases the sables in *Gorky Park.*

Citizen Kane (1941). Who can forget the opening scene, where all we see is Kane's mouth muttering "Rosebud" through the snow in the glass globe? Of course, the reporters in the film never do figure out what the reference is to, but the viewer knows that Rosebud was Kane's sled during his childhood—a symbol of the last time he felt happiness.

It's a Wonderful Life (1946). George Bailey loses his hearing in one ear (thereby setting the entire course of his life in motion) when he rescues his brother, who accidently falls through the ice after sledding on a snow shovel. Years later George wrecks his car on a snow-slick bridge and runs through the falling snow back to his loving family to end the movie.

Lost Horizon (1937). Ronald Coleman's plane crashes in the snow of Tibet, in the mystical, utopian valley of Shangri-La. Unlike in the real world, the only rule here is kindness.

The Wizard of Oz (1939). While in the home stretch on their way to Oz, Dorothy and her traveling pals are drugged in a field of poppies by the Wicked Witch. Glinda makes it snow to awaken them so they can complete their journey.

The Gold Rush (1925). In this Charlie Chaplin classic, the Little Tramp finds himself in Alaska, trudging through the snow in search of gold and his sweetheart.

Meet Me in St. Louis (1944). Judy Garland and family

build a family of snow people that Margaret O'Brien destroys when she thinks they are moving away from their idyllic world in St. Louis.

Dr. Zhivago (1965). No film with Russia as a backdrop ever used snow more successfully. Think of Yuri and his family fleeing the Bolsheviks and arriving at their dacha in the country. It looks like a snow castle, completely covered with snow and ice.

Murder on the Orient Express (1974). A snowdrift blocking the railroad tracks gives Hercule Poirot the time to solve the mystery.

Downhill Racer (1969). In one of his breakthrough roles, Robert Redford stars as an enigmatic Olympic skier intent on capturing the gold medal for himself more than for his country.

Raiders of the Lost Ark (1981). Indiana Jones begins his search for the amulet, which will lead him to the ark, in Tibet, at a snow-glazed bar run by his former flame. During a brawl with the Nazis he brands a leather-coated SS man with the amulet, and the villian is forced to find relief in the nearest snowbank.

Around the World in 80 Days (1956). As Phileas Fogg and Passepartout begin their journey, they pass over the Alps and grab snow to chill the champagne they've brought for the ride.

Spellbound (1945). Gregory Peck is an amnesiac with a

recurring, haunting dream of parallel lines. Ingrid Bergman helps him recover his suppressed recollection using ski tracks in the snow to jar his memory of a fatal accident.

The Eiger Sanction (1975). Secret agent Clint Eastwood squints his way through this film that uses the incredible Eiger as background. The snow-covered mountain-climbing climax is the most thrilling part.

The Shining (1980). Talk about your snowbound settings! Jack Nicholson is at his creepiest in this Stephen King tale of a family terrorized at an out-of-season resort. Between the suspense and the snow, you won't stop shivering for a week.

Love Story (1970). Love means never having to say you're sorry for hitting your girlfriend in the face during a snowball fight.

101 Dalmations (1961). Pongo and Perdy and puppies escape from the deVil mansion in a blizzard, wiping their footprints away with branches, walking on ice and otherwise ingeniously escaping detection in the snow. The snow helps and hinders their escape, but of course everyone lives happily ever after (except Cruella).

Snow Bond

Snow has been a recurrent setting for Agent 007. The opening pretitle sequence in *The Spy Who Loved Me* (1977) features James Bond fleeing enemy agents over a glacier and making a narrow escape over the edge (literally) by employing a parachute (strategically adorned with the Union Jack). In *For Your Eyes Only* (1981) Bond escapes from the baddies through a crowded Swiss resort, on skis and snowmobiles. Perhaps Bond's most inventive escape through snow was in *The Living Daylights* (1987), in which he schusses down the slopes in a cello case.

By the way, fake snow is created on Hollywood sets with either rock salt on the ground (and table salt sprinkled on lapels for tight shots), plastic chips, or chopped feathers blown by fans.

Snow Songs

"Let It Snow"

"Frosty the Snowman"

"White Christmas"

"Winter Wonderland"

"Jingle Bells"

"The Sleigh Ride"

"Over the River and Through the Woods"

Snowy Characters

* Snowball was the name of the idealistic pig in George Orwell's novel *Animal Farm.*

* Snow White appeared in two separate fairy tales written by the Brothers Grimm. "Snow White and Rose Red" and "Snow White and the Seven Dwarfs."

CHAPTER 7

PRACTICALLY SNOW

It's beautiful while it's falling, terrific to play in and even tastes good (with the right seasoning). But snow can also be dangerous if you're not properly prepared. That means dressing right and remembering some basic safety tips.

Outdoor Clothing and Equipment

In very cold and snowy weather, two pairs of socks are recommended by snow pros—a light layer next to your skin to wick away perspiration, then a woolen layer for warmth.

Mittens are better than gloves—they keep fingers together and conduct heat over your whole hand by trapping air and allowing your fingers, as they move, to generate heat and warm one another (sorry, Thumbkin, you're on your own). They can also be made out of heavier material than gloves which keeps the weather away. Two mittens (a light knit pair under a thicker, warmer, waterproof pair) are an even toastier solution. (Inuit mittens are made with two thumbs so the mitten can be turned around if the palm is soaking wet.)

When your hands do get cold, do "windmills—" kind of like the arm movement of the backstroke—or warm them in your armpits. You can also raise them above your head and drop them forcefully by your side to get the blood flowing back down to your hands which will warm them up. If you watch skiers in competition as they wait around the top of the mountain, you'll see them whipping their arms around in these ways to stay warm.

About hats: your mother was right. They really do work to keep your entire body warm. Hats and hoods allow your body to pump warming blood not just to your cold noggin, but to your frozen extremities as well. Ears should be tucked in, too.

Neck gaiters (as opposed to leg gaiters) are knit tubes—turtlenecks sans shirt—that fit over the head and hug the neck. They can be pulled up to cover ears and faces, too.

A good sweater or parka should fit snugly at the waist, neck and wrists to seal in warmth. However, it should be loose enough to fit over layers of clothes without impeding movement.

Ideally, snow boots should be designed to keep water out and heat in. Soles should be made of rubber (or a synthetic such as PVC) and offer good traction. If uppers are not waterproof, a sealant such as Scotchguard or a product like Sno-Seal is a good bet. Boots should fit well—allowing toes to wiggle even in a pair of heavy weight socks. If you limit blood flow or circulation, you'll chill quickly. You can dry boots out by turning them upside down.

When in doubt, layer, layer, layer. The pockets of air that are trapped between the layers serve as additional insulation and help keep you warmer. If you're out playing in the snow and you get wet, layers also make it possible to strip off the wet outer clothes so that you can stay dry. Moisture is one of the worst contributors to chill.

Long underwear made of natural fibers (cotton or a cotton-wool blend) should go on first. An insulating layer (usually made of a synthetic fiber) that traps body heat without holding in moisture is next. An outer layer should block wind and wet. Layers of fluffy, loose-fitting clothes of cotton or wool are ideal, unless you're planning strenuous snow play. In that case, wear synthetic long underwear, such as polypropylene, to draw perspiration efficiently away from the body.

Ski clothes are not just brightly colored for fashion (although there's no denying that fashion is a big selling point with some skiers). Bright colors absorb heat. Most Arctic flowers are bright pink, purple or yellow for this reason.

If you're doing serious snow hiking or for even better traction when shoveling your driveway, invest in a pair of crampons; they're like tire chains for your feet. Crampons provide improved traction, especially going uphill, by digging into the snow and ice. Ski poles enable your to keep better balance and find secure footing.

Sunglasses in the winter? Actually the glare of sun reflecting off snow can be more dangerous to your eyes than the summer's rays. The reflected ultraviolet radiation is so intense that it can burn your corneas. This is known as snow blindness. Snow blindness is extremely painful, and those who have experienced it liken the sensation to sand in their eyes.

Serious mountain climbers wouldn't venture outdoors without their shades, including the kind with the leather shields on the side (sometimes called glacier glasses) to protect against peripheral UV rays. Wear sunglasses even on gray days, especially at high altitudes. If you didn't bring your shades, make a pair of snow goggles from a piece of cardboard or even paper with narrow slits to see through. Tie them on with a piece of string or extra shoelace.

First Aid

The most important medical advice for the snow is fairly obvious: use common sense to avoid prolonged exposure to the cold and the wet and you'll stay in one piece. Snow itself seems very benign, even peaceful, but when combined with low temperatures and windchill it can prove deadly.

I'm Snow Cold

Frostbite occurs after prolonged exposure to cold, when tissue begins to deteriorate as a result of decreased blood circulation. It usually begins in extremities (fingers and toes) and then moves to larger parts of the body. If not treated properly, it can result in serious injury. The first visible signs of frostbite are white spots on the skin (especially the tip of your nose and cheeks). One key to treating frostbite is slowly warming up the frostbitten areas, as application of extreme heat can cause more damage to the tissue. And don't pay any attention to that old wives' tale that rubbing frostbite with snow is a cure—it's very dangerous! To avoid frostbite, cover exposed areas with mittens, hats and scarves. Even short exposure in the bitter cold can result in injury. Also keep moving, as blood circulating through your entire body will warm you up.

More serious than frostbite is hypothermia, a lowering of the body's core temperature below 95°F. This occurs after prolonged exposure to cold temperatures, and most often occurs as the result of an accident, such as falling through thin ice into a frozen lake or being trapped in an avalanche. If you're not absolutely sure about the thickness of ice, don't even think about skating, skimobiling or even walking on it. If you're skiing or hiking in the mountains, especially after a fresh snowfall, be aware of avalanche lines and traverse the terrain with that in mind. Hypothermia requires immediate medical attention. Wrap the victim in warm layers and get them to a first aid station or emergency room as soon as possible.

Avalanches

Racing down a mountainside, an avalanche is snow at its fiercest and most destructive. In snow country, avalanches are serious business, and while it is an inexact science, conditions are monitored and every effort is made to predict these events.

Listen to and obey warnings at ski areas and when hiking. Most avalanches occur on steep slopes during or shortly after a heavy snowfall. Snowballs rolling down a steep slope are a tip-off that the snow is unstable.

Anything can set off a deadly avalanche, from a yodel to a ski cutting into a steep slope. When skiing "off-piste" (off a marked trail), skiers should wear a "peepsie" (a transmitter about the size of a pocket knife). It peeps if you get snowed under and helps rescuers find you. It can also be switched to work as a receiver if you're doing the rescuing.

If you hear an avalanche heading down the mountain, pros suggest you head immediately to the outer edge of the oncoming snow and debris. If you can, grab onto a rock or tree when you reach the edge. If you can't anchor yourself to anything, try to take off anything that could cartwheel and hurt you (skis, packs, poles). When the wave of snow hits, "swim" with the flow and try to keep at the surface and toward the side. Keep your mouth closed when under the snow and, as you slow, try to clear a pocket in front of your face. When you stop, try to push upward through the snow with a hand (if you can't tell up from down, use gravity: spit). If you should find yourself stuck under the snow, rest quietly to conserve air and energy until rescued. In unusual *National Enquirer*-type cases, people have lived for several days; however, few people survive longer than a few hours.

Don't try to be a hero: direct descents don't always work, because the avalanche might well outrun you.

If you can, help find people swept away by snow. Keep them in sight as long as you can. Make careful note of where you saw them go under and start looking below that marker.

Snow Caves and Shelters

If you do get caught in snow country far from a cabin or Holiday Inn, don't panic. You can make yourself a shelter out of the snow. It works on the principle of an igloo: once the shelter is in place, the snow insulates you and protects you from freezing temperatures and winds.

Begin on the side of a hill or mountain since the incline provides you with one ready-made wall. Gently dig a hole in the snow to form a small cave. Remember to keep the walls thick enough to prevent collapse.

BLIZZARD ADVICE

The way to survive being stuck outside in a blizzard is not to fight it. According to Vilhjalmur Stefansson, author of the 1913 autobiography *My Life with the Eskimos,* Eskimos hunker down before they become physically exhausted or psychologically spent.

His advice, while waiting for improved visibility, is to:

1. Move only enough to keep warm. Working up a sweat dampens clothing and makes you colder.
2. Improvise a wind break out of the snow and try to sit out of the wind.
3. Sleep to conserve strength.

Modern survival techniques suggested by specialists may differ, so read up before engaging in winter camping.

Snow Tires

Since most of us have now progressed from dogsleds and sleighs to motorized transport, we've replaced one set of problems (dogs and horses tiring) for another (the need for snow tires and traction control). The following fundamentals come in handy.

The best advice for driving in snow is simple: *don't.* Of course, since most of us need to go to work, school, and the video store, we can't avoid driving. Drive smart. Obviously, try to stay on roads that have been well plowed. Even if you have a four-wheel drive vehicle, there's no need to be a Rambo.

Keep your distance. The more room you've got around you, the greater the margin for error for you and the other guy. Keep it slow no matter how impatient the person behind you may be. (If he or she is tailgating, turn on your flashers—that'll slow almost anyone down!) Don't pull any sudden moves—the idea is to keep the treads of your tires digging into the snow at all times. If you do start to skid, remember the words of your driver's ed instructor: *Steer into the skid*—don't try to fight it.

Just as important as knowing how to react in snow is knowing how to get out of it. There are several key items to keep in your car during the winter months:

* Shovel

* Bag of sand or cat litter

* Brush/scraper for windows

The operative concept here is *rock and roll.* No matter how powerful your car's engine, or whether it's got front- or rear-wheel drive, the only way to build momentum out of snow is to gently rock the car back and forth until it clears the snow under the tires.

First, dig out the snow from in front of the wheels and underneath the chassis. Spread some sand or even cat litter in front of each wheel. Then put the car in drive (or first if it's a stick shift) and give it a little gas. Just a little! Too much and you're just spinning your wheels—literally. Quickly put your foot on the brake and shift into reverse and gently step on the gas again. Contrary to some opinions, you should be sure to step on the brake while you're shifting gears. If you don't, you'll do a number on your transmission. The rocking motion uses the weight of the car to eventually propel it out of the snow. Of course, it doesn't hurt if some saintly friend, neighbor or passerby helps by giving the car a push while you're rocking.

A word on tires. Many people think that radials will get them by, even in the snow. But if you know that you're going to be doing a lot of driving in the snow, and must be able to get around, invest in a full set of radial snow tires. You can get ones with metal studs to maximize their effect, but check to make sure they're permitted in your area. Short of that, you can get a set of tire cables that will help increase traction.

Shoveling Out

As beautiful as snow may be while it's falling, there's no more dreaded activity than shoveling it. There's always the shortcut of calling the local snowplow operator and paying the usurious price for plowing your driveway. Or there's the more reasonable rate charged by the neighborhood "have shovel will travel" kids.

But most people have to tackle their drives and sidewalks themselves. Many of these same people can barely move the next day because of sore muscles and strained backs. Here are some tips on how to shovel properly.

* Invest in a good snow shovel—one that's wide and shallow and can move the maximum amount of snow with each shovelful.

* Wear good heavy gloves and clothing in layers. You're sure to work up a sweat, and it's a good idea to have layers that you can peel off during the shoveling process.

* BEND YOUR KNEES!. It's the same physical motion as any kind of lifting. The more of the load your legs carry, the less strain on your back.

* Take it easy. Wet, heavy snow can really tax your energy (not to mention your heart and respiratory system if you're the least bit out of shape). Everyone wants to finish as fast as possible, but take frequent rests.

* If you're home for the day, don't wait until after the snow has stopped to shovel. Shovel as soon as an inch or two has accumulated. The less snow on the drive or walk, the less in your shovel.

* Don't try to shovel ice. First break it up with the edge of your shovel, hoe or ice chipper. Then you can shovel away the pieces.

* If you live in a traditionally snowy area, think about

investing in a snow blower. These machines, similar to power lawn mowers, employ heavy blades that chop up the snow and blow it off to the side of the area you're working. They make short work of shoveling and pay for themselves quickly when you can stop calling the plow guy.

CHAPTER 8
SNOW KIDS

Snow and kids were made for one another. Most of the time they can roll around in it without getting dirty, eat it without getting sick and fall in it without getting hurt. Snow packs, molds, hurls, softens, flies, transforms and endlessly entertains. Who could ask for more? And as long as there are snowsuits, mufflers, mukluks and mittens that turn kids into Michelin men, there is much fun to be had in them thar drifts. So insist on a bathroom stop BEFORE the layers go on!

What Is Snow? (Kids' Version)

Snow, like ice, is made of frozen water. It's made of tiny drops of water that hang in the air. When it's warm, these droplets are rain. When the air is cold enough (around 32°F), the droplets begins to harden and stick together, making sleet. When the temperature drops even more, the water freezes into teeny ice crystals, also known as snow. Snow crystals come in many shapes and sizes but almost all have six sides. Next time it snows, go outside with a magnifying glass and a piece of dark colored construction paper. Catch some snowflakes on the paper and look at them through the magnifier. (See Chapter One for more details.)

Snow Fun
When it's OK to go outside

Before kids head out for a day in the snow, remember that they need sun and wind protection in the form of sunscreen and petroleum jelly applied to exposed skin. Give kids their own little tubes to keep in their pockets to prevent chapping.

One of the most fun things to do in freshly fallen snow is to make a snow angel. Lay down in untrodden snow with feet and legs together and arms by your side. Now, with elbows locked, swish your arms, fully extended, above your head and down to your side several times. Keeping your legs straight, spread them outward and then bring them together again. Do this action a few times. Without disturbing the snow any more, stand up carefully and admire your angel in the snow.

Nothing tastes better than a fresh snowflake, even if it's picked up a bit of pollution on its way through the atmosphere. To catch snowflakes on your tongue, point your chin at the sky, stick out your tongue and wait.

Chasing them around with your eyes trained skyward is asking for trouble, though.

Try an experiment. With a thermometer, test the temperature on top of the snow and then beneath it. Temperatures on the surface can be fifty degrees colder than beneath seven inches of snow. Old snow is dense because the ends of the crystals have been knocked off, making hard, round pellets. When snow becomes very dense and packed, it's called firn. Eventually, firn becomes glacial ice but that takes a lot of time. Now you've proven that snow is a good insulator.

Sandbox toys, food coloring, and kitchen molds are good tools for playing in the snow. They provide a way to build a sandcastle during the winter months.

An easy game for kids is Follow in the Leader's Footsteps, particularly for children of varied ages. The wider apart the steps the more fun!

And what better time of year than winter to play Frisbee? The great thing about this game in fluffy snow is that you can turn yourself into an acrobat trying to make spectacular catches without getting hurt.

Older children can construct a fort. Either cut blocks of hard-packed snow into bricks or use a cardboard box or wooden crate as a mold. Pack the bricks or unmolded blocks of snow one atop the other.

HOW TO MAKE A PERFECT SNOWMAN

Start with a good-sized, hard-packed snowball. Place it on the ground and roll it along, so that it picks up more snow as it goes. Make this first snowball pretty big since this will serve as your base. Repeat the process with another snowball but stop a bit sooner to create the middle of your snowman, and one more time, stopping even sooner, for his head.

Now you're ready to put Frosty together. Scoop a little bowl out on the top of the big ball to hold the next one. Carefully lift the medium-sized ball into place atop the big one. You may want to add a bit of snow where they join to make the structure more stable. When you're sure that these two aren't going anywhere, gently lift the head into place and fasten it the same way.

You can make your snowman come to life by using common household things for eyes (cookies, marbles, old tennis balls), noses (carrots, bananas) and mouths (any combination of the above). If you add an old hat and scarf, you'll have a classic

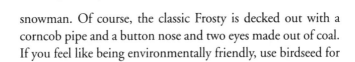

snowman. Of course, the classic Frosty is decked out with a corncob pipe and a button nose and two eyes made out of coal. If you feel like being environmentally friendly, use birdseed for hair and crackers for eyes—the birds will love you for it.

SNOWMAN TIPS: Pack the snow as tightly as you can to make your snowman last longer; hard-packed snow doesn't melt as fast as the snow on the ground. To make him last even longer, hose your snowman down with a fine spray of water to give him an icy overcoat. Don't worry if your snowman starts to melt in the sun—he'll freeze up again overnight.

SNOWMAN ALTERNATIVES: If the traditional shape doesn't do it for you, try sculpting a robot, mermaid, owl, airplane or superhero.

What's Inuit for Me?

People native to the Arctic call themselves *Inuit* (which translates as "the people") rather than Eskimos. There are many different Inuit nations; a single Inuit person is called an *Inuk*.

An igloo (Inuit for "house") is built by outlining a circle in the snow, along with a tunnel for the door (imagine a key hole). The first bricks of snow are carved for the tunnel area. Each brick should be slightly angled so the igloo will be dome-shaped. Make bricks smaller as you get to the top of the dome. Cut the snow from within the rising dome, leaving some snow for seating. Remember to always supervise children when building igloos or forts, just in case the structure collapses.

Kidski

Children as young as four can enroll in some ski schools, such as the program SKIwee, founded by *Ski* magazine and available at many ski resorts.

When renting ski equipment for kids, go to a reputable dealer. Skis should come roughly to the child's shoulder and should have brakes and well-tuned bindings with three-way releases. Boots should fit snugly but allow toes to wiggle. Ski poles, if recommended, should have flat (not pointed) tips and grips without straps.

A great way to start off on the right ski is in a children's ski (or snowboarding) school with instructors who make it fun and know their business. With older kids, make sure they know the rules of the mountain, are equipped with a trail map and understand that they may not ski or snowboard alone and must stay on clearly marked trails.

If your children are snowboarding, make sure they understand how to get on and off lifts and to keep their "leash" on to prevent runaway boards. Also make sure your little snowboarder's boots are waterproof and provide proper ankle support.

If the child seems to be having a rough time on skis or board, remember that even young children can snowshoe. Child-sized models can be rented or purchased and are worn with sturdy snow boots. And they needn't be made of wood and rawhide, as new, lightweight models are fashioned from aluminum tubing and synthetic straps.

Libby's Advice for Skiing with Kids

* Check first before selecting a resort for a family vacation. Find out about lodge childcare and whether reservations are required in advance for either childcare or ski school.

* Don't expect them to love it right away.

* If they're cold, let them warm up.

* Hot chocolate is good for morale.

* Ski school works.

* Nifty ski accessories are excellent enticements.

* Leasing skis for the season saves time.

Going Downhill Fast

If you let them, most kids can spend an entire day zipping downhill on some sledlike means of transport. There are two long-standing designs:

Toboggans are the modern relatives of the primitive sleds dragged by North American and Asian peoples to transport food, wood, furs and other commodities. While sleds with runners are better on hard-packed or shallow snow, toboggans are best in deep fluffy snow. There are few faster ways to plummet down a hill than on the smooth-bottomed toboggan, but beware: steering is an acquired art (accomplished by leaning one way or the other) and can't be counted on for too much accuracy. Stay away from trees, rocks and especially roads.

Originally called "coasters," *sleds* are a cross between a toboggan and a sleigh. Made of a wooden platform on steel runners, they can careen down hills at great speed and allow riders to stay relatively dry in the process. The Rolls-Royce of sleds in the twentieth century has always been the Flexible Flyer. Originally manufactured and patented by S. L. Allen & Company in Philadelphia, it was "the sled that steers."

Sledding Tips

When it's time to whip out the old Flexible Flyer or flying saucer, keep the following in mind to make your day on the hill an enjoyable one for everyone:

* Always give equipment a safety check. Make sure the sled, toboggan or whatever you're riding is in good condition.

* Don't put small children on downhill rides as passengers— it's dangerous.

* Don't sled around traffic.

* Check the course for hazards such as icy patches, large rocks, jagged twigs, looping vines, bumps, tree stumps or rough spots.

* Don't stand up. Only older kids should be allowed to "bel-lywhop," and try to dissuade them if you can. Also, leave the luge position to trained lugers.

* Don't lie motionless after falling off a sled and give everyone heart failure.

* Teach kids to be sure the course is clear before sliding off and to get out of the way quickly at the bottom of the hill.

* Walk back up the hill on the side, away from oncoming sleds.

* Whine at the bottom of the hill so a grown-up will drag the sled back to the top.

* Alternatives to sleds: cafeteria trays, suitcases, flattened cardboard, inner tubes, air mattresses, and, in a pinch, your backside in a snowsuit.

When It's Just Too Snowy to Go Outside

There are some snow days when the windchill is just too low (at least by parental standards) to venture out. Sometimes it's just wise to let the snow fall and gather before going out to play. For those days, some indoor activities are in order.

Try this science experiment: fill up same-sized containers with water, ice and snow. See how much of each it takes to produce the same amount of liquid. Does ice and snow really take up as much room as water?

Play Sir Hillary: stack up all the pillows and cushions in the house and try to climb to the summit.

Make paper snowflakes by cutting a sheet of white paper in a circle. (If you like, trace a circle using a bowl or plate). Fold the circle in half and then fold it again into three equal parts, making one shape that looks like a slice of pizza. Hold the pizza slice in one hand and, using scissors, cut little designs into the edges. Open up the paper to see how your snowflake is coming.

Make a bird feeder. Roll a pinecone in peanut butter and

then bird seed and hang it outside—or just tie some suet to a tree by your window. Remember that if you start feeding the birds, you have to continue all winter because they become dependent on your food as their only nourishment. Sprinkle birdseed or crumbled toast on the sill or on the snow and wait by a window for the birds and squirrels.

If all else fails, go for the pun. How about a game of Freeze Dancing? One player is in charge of the music and can stop and start it as he or she likes. Everyone has to freeze when the music suddenly stops. Or Freeze Tag: Players have to freeze in place when they're tagged.

All Snowed Out

Hot chocolate is to a snowy day what a snow cone is to a beachy day. To make it from scratch, pour a dribble of real milk into a mug and add a teaspoon of cocoa and a teaspoon of sugar. Mix it into a syrup at the bottom of the mug while more milk is warming in a saucepan. Pour the warm milk into the mug, stir thoroughly and add marshmallows as icebergs.

Now curl up with a snow story and warm your toes by the fire (or under a nice cozy blanket). A snowy day library for wee ones should include at least one of the following:

I Am a Bunny by Ole Risom and Richard Scarry

A Snowy Day by Ezra Jack Keats

Katy and the Big Snow by Virginia Lee Burton

The Snowman by Raymond Briggs

How the Grinch Stole Christmas by Dr. Seuss

One, Two, One Pair! by Bruce McMillan

Mama, Do You Love Me? by Barbara M. Joosse

Polar Bear, Polar Bear by Bill Martin, Jr.

A Winter's Day by Douglas Florian

Angelina Ice Skates by Katherine Holabird

The Little House on the Prairie series by Laura Ingalls Wilder

Little Polar Bear by Hans de Beer

White Snow, Bright Snow by Alvin Tresselt

The Snow Queen by Hans Christian Andersen

The Snow Maiden, a traditional fairy tale

CHAPTER 9

Snow to Speak

The properties and qualities of snow have contributed greatly to our linguistic store of adjectives, figures of speech and clichés. Snow has been used to characterize many things, from electronic interference on our television screens to virginal purity. Since the first caveman uttered "ugh" (probably upon waking to discover his wheel under a mound of snow) snow has been a popular descriptive word.

There are thousands of references, dating back to the first written words. Snow is used as a metaphor for cold, thick, white, pure, chaste, clear, fair, clean, feathered or unsullied. Claims that snow will melt, shine, fly away, disappear, vanish, gather by rolling, act as a fertilizer, or be welcome have been used in many a poetic turn of phrase.

A Blizzard of Words

Because snow and ice come to the Great White North in so many forms, there are a variety of words to describe the subtle differences.

According to Bill Bryson, author of *Mother Tongue,* Eskimos do indeed have fifty words for types of snow. (There are even more for ice.) Where snow plays such an important part in one's daily life as well as in a people's past and future, it makes sense that there would be words to differentiate varieties of it. Bryson claims that "curiously [there is] no word for just plain snow." But how odd is the many-words-for-snow phenomenon? Italians have more than five hundred words for different shapes of pasta, and Arabs have literally thousands of words for camels and camel accoutrements. And while we're on the subject, New Yorkers easily have as many words meaning idiot, while Californians have an entire thesaurus devoted to variations on dysfunctional.

Inuit words for types of snow include the following:

annui: falling snow

api: snow not yet driven by wind

det-thlok: break out the snowshoes if you think you're going to walk on this stuff *natatgonaq:* snow surface of rough particles

qali: snow that sticks to tree branches as it falls

qanittaq: new-fallen snow

saluma roaq: smooth snow crust of fine flakes

siqoq: snow resembling smoke that blows along the ground

upsik: snow altered by the wind into hard mass

There are also separate words for snow on the ground, soft snow on the ground, wet falling snow, drifts of hard snow or soft snow, crystalline snow on the ground, hard crusts of snow that give way to footfall, melting snow used as cement for a snow house, and so on. It's really not so strange a notion to have a specific word for each variant of the white stuff. Russians also have many words to describe different types of snow.

Snow has inspired a language all its own, affected by moisture content, temperature, geography, sun-glazing, thawing, refreezing, wind, overuse and so on. Ski resorts classify slopes, for example, as hard-packed, loose granular, frozen granular, machine groomed, wet granular, wet packed, spring conditions, variable conditions, wind-blown and ice.

Other variations of snow and snowlike conditions include the following:

cement: moisture-heavy, unwieldy, gloppy snow

corn: common in spring, large grains of snow formed after several cycles of freezing and thawing

crud: a catch-all term for snow that is difficult to ski on because it's a mixture of broken crust, ice and soft snow

crust: a layer of hard snow atop softer snow which may or may not be able to support your weight

granular snow: snow made up of large, coarse crystals

neve: hard, well-consolidated granular snow

powder: light, dry snow that has not yet been compacted (usually because it's new-fallen)—the fluffiest variety is a skier's idea of paradise, while the wetter kind is like skiing through mashed potatoes

snowsnakes: unseen, nonexistent "things" that stretch beneath the surface of snow ready to trip you up, tangle your skis, force a headfirst fall, or simply separate you from the ground for no good reason *transition snow:* unpredictable snow when the temperature is just hovering at the freezing point

whiteout: when windblown, thickly falling snow makes visibility so difficult you cannot tell the ground from the sky or, sometimes, the mitten in front of your nose

Other formulations and definitions of snow and the snow-related include these:

arete: a narrow ridge of snow and/or rock

cornice: a big curl of wind-shaped snow that looks like a breaking wave and forms on promontories and cliffs (because they usually dramatically overhang their rock base, avoid hiking or skiing on one)

crevasse: a deep split in the surface of a glacier which may or may not be visible

cup crystals: oversized cup-shaped crystals in snowpack that foretell of possible avalanches (also known as depth hoar)

firn: akin to neve, compacted granular snow

fjord: a Norwegian word for a narrow ocean inlet cutting between steep slopes or cliffs—spectacularly beautiful when snow-covered

frost: a thin layer of ice made from water droplets that forms on a surface

graupel: rounded ice crystals, like soft hail, that may form an unstable layer in the snowpack, leading to avalanche

hail: precipitation in the form of chunks or nuggets that is most typically a layering of ice and dense snow around a frozen core (such as a raindrop or pellet of soft hail)

hoar: similar to white, crystalline frost

moguls: hard bumps of snow on a downhill trail

rime: a crusty feathering of snow or frost that forms on an object from a cloud or supercooled fog and wind

sastrugi: drifts blown by the wind that resemble waves or ridges

serac: a thick column of snow or ice found in or beside an icefall

sleet: precipitation in the form of small, irregular ice pellets developing from rain when the temperature falls near 32°F and raindrops harden and stick together (below 32°F, it changes to snow)

slush: wet snow (and, colloquially, overt or aggressive sentimentality) *snowball:* 1. a ball made out of hard-packed snow 2. as a verb, to increase rapidly in size and/or speed 3. to overwhelm and sudue or crush

sublimation: the process whereby a speck of dust or dirt envelops itself in a water molecule and changes the molecule from vapor to an ice crystal or snow

windslab: a thick layer of snow that forms on the lee side of slopes

Snow Slang

Our vocabulary is rich in snow expressions and slang, young and old:

flake: originally a baseball term for an oddball, or, more kindly, a colorful individualist

nova under snow on a sled: once lunch-counter shorthand for smoked salmon and cream cheese on an English muffin

slush fund: a political term for a cache of money used for questionable dealings (this dates back to an age-old military tradition of creating a fund from the sale of unimportant surplus to buy little luxuries for the troops or crew)

slush pump: slang for a jazz trombone

snow: 1. since the early 1900s, a street name for cocaine or heroin 2. used as a verb, to persuade someone, using shameless hyperbole, flattery and exaggeration, in a doubtful cause (a century ago it meant to overwhelm with excessive orders or demands) 3. to purposefully deceive 4. nineteenth-century slang for clean linens hanging on the line to bleach dry in the sun (and someone who stole laundry off the line was a snow-gatherer)

snowball's chance in hell: no way—completely impossible

snowbird: once a turn-of-the-century expression for a migratory worker headed south for the winter or someone who enlisted in the army during the winter months (presumably for sustenance) and deserted in the spring. It's now used, particularly in the Southwest and Florida, for northerners who "fly" south to escape cold and snow

snow bunny: 1. a young person (who may or may not actually ski) hanging around a ski resort 2. once, a Royal Marine trained in Arctic warfare

snowed in or *up:* under the influence of cocaine

snow job: an expression popularized by the armed forces

in the 1940s, trying with enormous effort to persuade someone (as in *to snow someone*)

"snow again—I didn't get your drift": 1950s Canadian slang for "please repeat that, I didn't hear you"

snow broth: slang for cold tea

snow-puncher: World War I British slang for a Canadian soldier

snow rupee: a century-old colloquialism from India for a genuine rupee (Indian money)

snowball hitch: Military slang for a knot that easily comes adrift

snowdrop: World War II military slang for white-helmeted military police

snowed in or *under:* 1. overburdened with work or overwhelmed with things to do 2. New Zealand sheep shearers' expression for working so fast that the shorn fleece piles up to the workers' chins

"snowing down south" or *"snowing in France":* archaic school kids' phrase meaning your petticoat or slip is showing